Ol'
Clip-Clop

A Ghost Story

by **Patricia C. McKissack**

illustrated by
Eric Velasquez

Holiday House / New York

To James Everett McKissack,
who loves horses
—P. M.

To all the victims
and survivors
of Hurricane Sandy,
2012
—E. V.

Text copyright © 2013 by Patricia McKissack
Illustrations copyright © 2013 by Eric Velasquez
All Rights Reserved
HOLIDAY HOUSE is registered in the U.S. Patent and Trademark Office.
Printed and Bound in April 2013 at Tien Wah Press,
Johor Bahru, Johor, Malaysia.
The text typeface is Gryphius.
The artwork was created with mixed media and oil on watercolor paper.
www.holidayhouse.com
First Edition
Library of Congress Cataloging-in-Publication Data
McKissack, Pat, 1944-
Ol' Clip-Clop : a ghost story / by Patricia C. McKissack ; illustrated by Eric Velasquez. — 1st ed.
p. cm.
Summary: One October night, John Leep, a mean and stingy landlord, sets out to evict
a widow from one of his rental houses and is followed by a ghostly rider.
ISBN 978-0-8234-2265-4 (hardcover)
[1. Ghosts—Fiction. 2. Conduct of life—Fiction.]
I. Velasquez, Eric, ill. II. Title.
PZ7.M478693Ol 2011
[E]—dc22
2010029448

The year was 1741. The month was October.
The day was Friday the thirteenth.

John Leep closed his law office earlier than usual. He had something to do that made him smile.

Smiling didn't come easy to a man like John Leep. He had a mean streak in him that ran the length of his long, thin body.

Wasn't poverty that made him hard. He had plenty of money.

But John Leep had a stingy heart. Worse still, not one of the three hundred residents of Grass Hollow—not one—called him friend.

But on this particular night he had nothing on his mind except evicting the widow Mayes, who lived in one of his rental houses. He'd decided not to wait until morning; it was much better to put her out at night.

"This will be an example for all my other tenants," he grumbled. "Pay rent on time or get put out. Ha-ha!"

Mounting his horse, Major,
John Leep set out to do his deed.
Clip. Clop. Clip. Clop.
At first the lamps along the
street lit the way. A dog howled
in the distance, a stray cat
scurried up a nearby tree, and his
horse's hooves clanked against
the cobblestone street. *Clip.
Clop. Clip. Clop.*

It was a moonless night, cold even for October, yet John Leep
was warmed by the idea of evicting the widow Mayes and raising the
rent on his property without fixing it up. *Clip. Clop. Clip. Clop.*

But wait.
Listen. Behind him he heard
another set of hooves striking the
cobblestones. *Clip. Clop. Clip. Clop.*
John Leep paused under a street
lamp. "Hello," he called. Peering into
the darkness, he waited for the other
rider to come within the circle of
light to be recognized.
But no one appeared.

And so John Leep rode on. *Clip. Clop. Clip. Clop.*

At the north side of the village, he came to a dirt path that led to the lowlands of Grass Hollow. *Clip. Clop. Clip. Clop. Clip. Clop.*

Listen again.

He heard the muffled sound of another horse's hooves against the packed dirt. Someone was following.

Clip. Clop. Clip. Clop. Clip. Clop. John stopped; the other rider stopped too.

John called out, "If you are a robber, let me warn you that I am a skilled swordsman. You won't have a chance against me!" Poised and ready, he waited.

But no one came.

A blast of wind whipped at John Leep's cloak, chilling him to the core. *It's just some prankster trying to scare me. I'll not give him the satisfaction of seeing me frightened.* Still, he thought, it might not hurt to push Major to go a bit faster. *Clip-clip clop. Clip-clip clop.*

The invisible rider fell into step. *Clip-clip clop. Clip-clip clop.*

John Leep stopped again, waited and listened. Nothing.

Major pawed at the ground nervously, his nostrils flaring as puffs of frosty air escaped. Then from inside the heavy shadows Leep heard the impatient pawing of another steed.

"Go!" shouted John, slapping Major on the side. The horse took off!
Clip-clippity clop. Clip-clippity clop.

The other rider stayed with them. *Clip-clippity clop. Clip-clippity clop.*

John Leep tore down Peach Tree Hill, past the church, past the old cemetery, right up to the widow Mayes's front door. *Clip-clippity clop. Clip-clippity clop. Clip-clippity clop.*

"Open the door. Open up!" he yelled. "Now!"

"My goodness," said the widow Mayes, letting John Leep come in. "I know why you're here." She held up a bag of coins. "This is all the money I owe you."

"All of it?"
John Leep mumbled
unhappily. His hands
were still shaky, so
when he snatched
the bag, he
dropped it.

The widow
hurried to
gather the money.
She didn't see
John Leep hide a
coin in his boot.

"You're short. This isn't everything you owe me! You have to go. Pack your things and get out now! Go, go, go!" He scoffed.

"Oh, please," begged the widow Mayes. "I know I had all the rent money. Please let me stay the night."

Oooooooo. The wind rattled the door and shook the windows.

John Leep was clearly disturbed by the restless wind. He cried out, "You can stay till morning. I'll be back to put you out—first thing . . . unless you have all my money."

John Leep chuckled to himself. He knew the widow Mayes wasn't going to find the other coin. And nobody could say that he had been . . . unfair.

He rushed out. As he mounted Major, John Leep never realized that the coin hidden in his boot had fallen out and was waiting to be found by the widow Mayes as soon as she opened her front door the next morning.

Was that laughter he heard?

"Who are you? What do you want?" John Leep yelled.

The wind whispered a chilling response. *Weeeee! Yoooooooou!*

John Leep pushed Major to run as fast as possible.
Clippity-cloppity, clippity- cloppity, clippity-cloppity.
Faster still. *Clippitycloppity. Clippitycloppity.*
Clippitycloppity. John Leep rode on—along the river and
across the bridge. But the phantom rider followed relentlessly.
Clippitycloppityclippitycloppityclippitycloppityclippity. . . .
"Faster! Go faster!" John Leep yelled.
Clippitycloppityclippitycloppityclippitycloppityclippity cloppity.
At last he burst through the darkness. Major's
horseshoes struck fire from the cobblestones.
*Clippitycloppityclippitycloppityclippitycloppityclippity
cloppity.* Just a few more feet and he'd be home.
Clippitycloppityclippitycloppityclippitycloppityclippity cloppity.

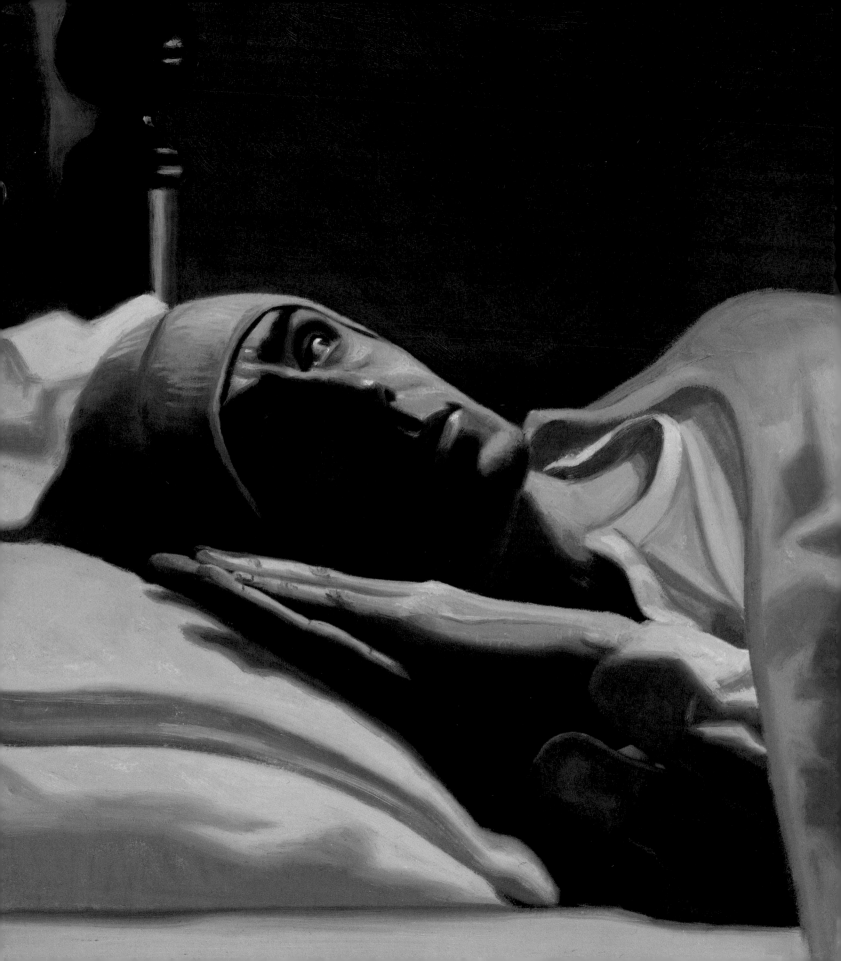

He made it!

While getting ready for bed, he chuckled. "I've been running from a mere echo. And now I'm exhausted."

He crawled into bed . . . and he was never seen again.

Whatever happened to John Leep that night? Nobody ever really knew. Strangest thing. He left Major behind, and the widow Mayes never heard from him again. Some said John Leep settled in another state, changed his ways, and was known for being kind and generous. But other people were convinced that Ol' Clip-Clop . . .

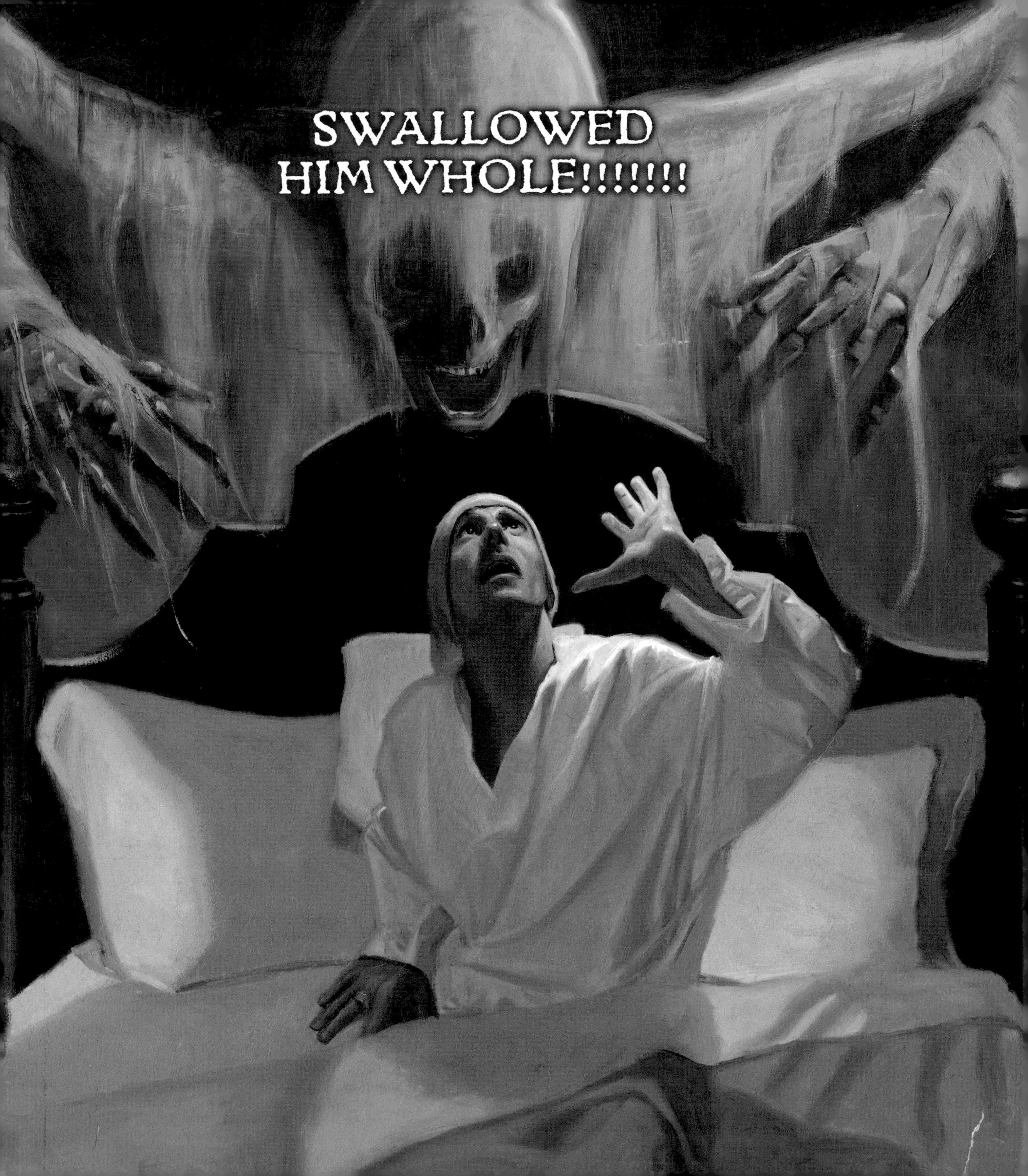
SWALLOWED
HIM WHOLE!!!!!!!